Miss Kitty, the New Baby, and Me

by Michael J. Pellowski

illustrated by Tammy Starner-Altop

"To my own little Melanie"

Published by Willowisp Press, Inc.
401 E. Wilson Bridge Road, Worthington, Ohio 43085

Printed in the United States of America

10 9 8 7 6 5 4 3 2

ISBN 0-87406-063-X

One

"KNOCK it off, Miss Kitty," scolded Melanie Parker. "Quit being a pain! You used to like to dress up." The little cat wiggled and squirmed as Melanie slipped a frilly doll gown over its head.

Miss Kitty blinked and settled down. She scrunched up her pink nose and pawed at her long white whiskers. Loudly, she sneezed once, twice, and then again.

"Bless you," Melanie said as she tied the strings of the gown. "These frills might tickle a little, but they make you look real cute."

Miss Kitty blinked slowly and stretched out lazily on the playroom couch. The couch was

Miss Kitty's special spot. She loved to take naps there.

Melanie folded her arms across her favorite T-shirt. It had the picture of a cartoon cat painted on the front. Melanie scratched her head and concentrated. "Now where did I leave the bonnet and booties that go with this gown?"

Remembering was no easy chore. Melanie and Miss Kitty had not played the dress-up game in a long time. That was because having tea parties, playing house, and dressing up were starting to seem just a bit corny. After all, Melanie was now nine years old going on ten. And there were lots of newer things to do—like experimenting with her mom's makeup for one.

But every once in a while the old games sounded like fun to Melanie. Maybe it was because she and Miss Kitty were such good friends. To Melanie, Miss Kitty was like a real person. She was someone Melanie could share secrets and dreams with. The two were a matched pair. They did everything together.

Melanie considered Miss Kitty a member of the family.

"Now I remember," Melanie told Miss Kitty. "I stuck a whole bunch of doll clothes in a cardboard box. And I stuck the box in the back of the closet."

Melanie bounded across the playroom floor, side-stepping clumps of books and stuffed animals. Neatness had never been one of her strong points.

As soon as Melanie reached the closet door Miss Kitty's ears perked up. When Melanie turned the knob, Miss Kitty popped to her feet. The playroom closet was one of the cat's secret hiding places. Another was behind the dresser in the playroom. The playroom was home base for Miss Kitty. She was accustomed to doing whatever she wanted to do in the playroom.

Melanie opened the door. Zap! Miss Kitty took off like an Olympic sprinter. Across the couch and over the dresser she scampered. Like a bolt of furry lightning, she flashed through Melanie's legs into the overstuffed closet.

"What the . . . ? Hey, watch it!" screeched Melanie. "Have you gone bonkers, or what?" Miss Kitty paid no attention to Melanie. The little cat shot straight to the back part of the closet. Melanie dropped to her knees and reached in.

"Come out of there," Melanie ordered. But Miss Kitty didn't appear. "Come out, or I'm coming in after you," Melanie called. Still, there was no Miss Kitty.

Melanie parted a row of winter coats hanging from the rack and crawled into the closet on her hands and knees. "Yuck! This closet smells musty," she said aloud.

Melanie held her nose and crept deeper into the dark closet. There in a far corner was Miss Kitty as proud as could be. In her mouth was a favorite toy. It was the catnip mouse Melanie had given Miss Kitty for Christmas.

"I wondered what you did with that mouse," Melanie said. She picked up Miss Kitty and started back out noticing the odor again. The closet really does smell bad, she thought.

"Someone should scrub out that closet with antiseptic," Melanie said to Miss Kitty. "I'd better tell Mom about it." Melanie stroked her pet's head. Miss Kitty began to purr in a contented way.

Holding Miss Kitty in her lap, Melanie pulled out the box of doll clothes. She tossed things here and there searching for the booties and bonnet she wanted. Finally, at the bottom of the box, she found them.

"Now hold still," she told Miss Kitty. This time Miss Kitty stayed quiet and calm. Melanie put booties on the cat's paws. She tied a bonnet on Miss Kitty's head. Then Melanie smiled and held up her pet for a last look.

"The toy mouse has to go," she announced, shaking her head. "Well-dressed babies in Smithville just don't go around with mice between their teeth." Melanie took the toy out of Miss Kitty's mouth. "That's better," she said.

Standing up, she hugged her pet. Miss Kitty purred loudly. Her paws went around Melanie's neck as if she were hugging Melanie back.

"Let's go outside. I want to show you off to Sandy."

Sandy Morgan and her parents lived next door to the Parkers. Sandy was a junior in high school. She was also Melanie's babysitter. Melanie felt close to Sandy, and Sandy liked Melanie, too. They were the only girls on the block. In fact, they were the only children in the neighborhood.

Melanie started to leave the room. She stopped and glanced back at the doll clothes all over the floor. "What a mess! We'll clean it up later," she said to Miss Kitty. "What the heck! It's only the playroom. Mom won't be mad."

Melanie was right. Her mother and father never complained about the playroom, even when it started to look like a disaster area. The extra room had been Melanie's ever since the Parkers moved to Smithville five years ago. It had always been a place where Melanie and Miss Kitty could have fun. Her parents let Melanie and her cat do whatever they wanted to do in the playroom.

"Hey, Mom," yelled Melanie as she carried Miss Kitty into the living room. As usual on Saturday afternoon, Melanie's dad was lying on the couch watching a ball game. After Mrs. Parker and Melanie, sports was his next love.

"Whoa! Not so loud, Mel. What's the problem?" Melanie's dad asked. "Why do you need your mother?"

"The closet stinks," Melanie replied.

Mr. Parker's left eyebrow rose. His eyebrows always gave away his thoughts. When he got mad or nervous they twitched in a funny fashion.

"What?" asked Mr. Parker as he sat up stiffly.

"The closet smells awful."

"Which closet?" asked Melanie's mother, entering the room.

"The playroom closet, Mom," explained Melanie. "It really smells terrible."

"I'll try to find time to clean it," Mrs. Parker said to Melanie.

"Samantha," Melanie's dad said to his wife. "I don't think it's a good idea to be doing that kind of work." He glanced nervously from his wife to his daughter. His eyebrows started to twitch. "I'll clean out the closet." He stood up and switched off the TV set.

"Dad's going to scrub out the closet? On Saturday? He's not going to watch the baseball game?" Melanie held Miss Kitty at arm's length and stared at her. "What's going on? Miss Kitty, are we in the right house?"

"Okay, cut the comedy," sputtered Mr. Parker. "I'll . . ."

Mrs. Parker interrupted. "I'll clean the closet, George." Then she turned to Melanie and said, "You've dressed up Miss Kitty. You haven't done that in a long time."

"Yeah, I know. I just felt like it," Melanie said. "I'm going over to the Morgans. I want to show Sandy how cute Miss Kitty looks." Melanie fondled Miss Kitty in her arms and headed for the front door.

"She carries that cat just like it's a real baby," George Parker said to his wife.

"It's good practice," Samantha Parker answered.

Mr. Parker smiled. "I can't wait to see the look on Mel's face when we finally tell her the news."

Mrs. Parker sat down. "I hope she won't feel threatened."

"What do you mean?" One eyebrow went up.

"Melanie has been an only child for nine, almost ten years," Mrs. Parker explained. "Suddenly she'll find out she's going to have a baby brother or sister. That'll mean sharing things she's never had to share before."

"Mel can handle it," Mr. Parker assured his wife. "Our girl is adaptable. Look how well she adapted to living in a neighborhood with no kids her own age."

"Miss Kitty had a lot to do with that," Mrs. Parker reminded her husband.

"That's true," he admitted. "She sure loves that cat."

Mrs. Parker exhaled loudly. "That's another problem. When we turn the playroom into the baby's nursery, what are we going to do with Miss Kitty? We can't have a cat running all over the place."

Mr. Parker stroked his chin thoughtfully. "I never gave it much thought. That could be a real problem. I like the cat. But if it's a question of the baby's security, the cat will have to go."

"Well," sighed Mrs. Parker. "Maybe we can work things out. We have almost seven months left." She smiled and stood up. "I might as well tackle that closet right now."

Mr. Parker clamped two fingers on his nose and pinched his nostrils shut. "Lead on," he joked. "I'm all ready to help. Stinky closets are a specialty of this new father-to-be. After all, we don't want our newest child to have a smelly nursery."

"Heaven forbid," teased Mrs. Parker as they walked away together.

Two

WITHIN a month Mrs. Parker began to look like an expectant mother. "George, I think it's time to have a talk with Melanie," Mrs. Parker said to her husband.

Mr. Parker gagged on his morning coffee and lowered the Sunday paper he was reading. "Already? Can't we wait a little longer?" he sputtered. "We haven't made a decision about Miss Kitty yet. Shouldn't we wait until we iron out the problem?"

"George Parker, how long do you think I can wait?" Mrs. Parker replied. "My clothes don't fit. I've got to start wearing maternity clothes soon."

"Couldn't we tell Melanie maternity clothes are a new fad or something?"

14

"Don't be ridiculous, George. Some people have already guessed I'm expecting a baby," Mrs. Parker said. "It's time for Melanie to know."

George Parker nodded in agreement. He folded his paper and laid it on the kitchen table. "Melanie, would you come out here please," he called.

Melanie was in the playroom. "I'll be right there, Dad. I want to finish reading the Sunday comics."

"All right. Come out when you're finished, honey," Mr. Parker said, trying to remain calm. He looked at his wife nervously. His eyebrows were beginning to tremble. He wanted to get the talk over with as quickly as possible.

Minutes later, Melanie appeared. "What's up?" she asked. She noticed her dad's eyebrows and smiled. "Good news or bad?" she asked as she flopped in a chair.

"We have something important to talk about," Mr. Parker began. "It has to do with your mom, but it concerns all of us."

"Uh-oh," joked Melanie. "What did you do, Mom, lose the checkbook or dent the car?"

"It's nothing like that, honey," Mrs. Parker replied. "It's . . . well, we may be getting a new addition to our family."

"A gerbil!" Melanie shouted jumping to her feet. "You know I always wanted a gerbil! Can I pick it out?"

Mr. and Mrs. Parker shifted uneasily in their seats. "It's not a gerbil, Melanie," said Mr. Parker scratching his head. "If you'll let us finish, maybe you'll find out what we're talking about."

Melanie raised her eyebrows, a trait she inherited from her dad. She dropped back into her chair and apologized. "Sorry, but you're sure it's not a gerbil, Dad? Miss Kitty and I would sure love having a gerbil."

"You'll love this even more," Melanie's father answered.

"At least I hope so," Mrs. Parker added with a sigh.

Melanie's dad continued. "Haven't you noticed

that your mother is gaining weight?" he asked his daughter.

"I know," Melanie said as she propped an elbow on the table and rested her chin in her hand. "I've dropped a million hints about diets, but she just won't listen. Mom, I told you, thin is in."

Melanie's dad got up and walked over to her mom. He put his arm around her. "This is the one time it's perfectly healthy for your mom to gain weight," he said. Mr. Parker kissed his wife on the cheek.

Melanie looked confused. She scratched her head in a puzzled way. "You two sure are acting goofy. My friend Tina at school told me when parents act goofy it means one of three things."

"What three things?" prompted Mrs. Parker.

"A wedding," said Melanie, "a divorce, or a new baby."

"Well, no one is getting married," said Mr. Parker with a snicker.

Melanie gulped and looked shocked. Her hands

gripped the table edge tightly. "Oh, no," she gasped, "not—not a divorce?"

"No, silly," said Mrs. Parker, "the other thing."

Melanie's jaw dropped open. "A baby?" she muttered. Mrs. Parker smiled and nodded.

"W-We're having a b-baby?" Melanie stammered.

"Well, actually I'm having the baby," corrected Mrs. Parker.

"A baby! All right!" yelled Melanie, jumping to her feet. "A baby! I'm going to have a baby sister!" Melanie rushed over and hugged her mother warmly.

"How about a hug for me?" pleaded Mr. Parker. "I had a little bit to do with this."

"Sure, Dad. You can have a hug, too." Melanie cried, giving her dad a big bear hug. "A baby sister. Wow!"

"Time out! Slow down, big sister," Melanie's father said. "The baby might be a boy. It could be George, Junior." Mr. Parker grinned proudly.

"Nah! Not a chance," Melanie said. "I know it. I can tell. Right, Mom?"

"We don't know," confessed Mrs. Parker. "Let's just hope the baby is healthy."

"I've got to tell Miss Kitty," shouted Melanie as she dashed from the kitchen. "We're going to be a family of five. Miss Kitty, we're getting a baby sister."

Melanie raced into the playroom. Miss Kitty was dozing in her favorite spot on the couch. Melanie stroked the sleeping cat. "Wake up, lazy bones! I've got big news," Melanie announced as she plopped down beside her pet.

Miss Kitty yawned and opened her eyes slowly. Melanie lifted her fluffy pet and placed the cat on her lap. "Guess what? Mom's having a baby. We're going to get a sister. Isn't that super?"

If Miss Kitty was excited over the news, she didn't show it. She lay still and began to purr quietly. But Melanie could barely control her enthusiasm.

"We're going to have a great time together, the three of us," Melanie said. "It'll be a blast. My new sister can have all my old toys. We'll share everything. We'll have so much fun."

Just then Melanie's mom and dad appeared in the doorway of the playroom. "I heard what you said about sharing," Mr. Parker said to Melanie. "Do you really mean it, honey?"

"Sure, dad. Why?"

"We were thinking about your playroom," Melanie's mom said.

"My playroom?" questioned Melanie. "What about it?"

"We were thinking the playroom would make a wonderful nursery for the baby," Mr. Parker explained.

Melanie was silent. She thought for a minute. Then she leaned over and whispered to Miss Kitty. "We don't mind, do we?" Miss Kitty didn't bat an eyelash.

Melanie looked up at her parents. "It would still be partially my room, right?"

Mr. and Mrs. Parker went over and hugged their daughter. "Of course," Mrs. Parker told Melanie as she sat down beside her. "Besides, who do you think is going to help change this from a messy playroom to a beautiful nursery?"

Melanie pointed at herself. "Me?"

"Certainly not your father," replied Melanie's mom.

"Thanks," teased Melanie's dad. "I guess I'm only good for helping clean out stinky closets." Mr. Parker held his nose and walked out pretending he was mad. "I guess I'll just have to go read the sports section," he said.

"May I really help decorate the nursery?" Melanie asked her mom.

"Yes, indeed," her mother answered. "With a new baby on the way, I'm counting on you to be my number one interior decorator."

"Boy! This is working out great," Melanie said to Miss Kitty. "Losing our playroom won't be so bad. Look what we're getting in return, a baby sister."

"It may be a boy," Mrs. Parker said.

Melanie wasn't really listening to her mother. She was already thinking about where the baby's crib should go, what color curtains would look best, and so on.

Miss Kitty finally woke up. She sprang off of Melanie's lap and sharpened her claws on the arm of the sofa. Then she bounded from the sofa to the dresser top.

Mrs. Parker watched Miss Kitty's antics with mixed emotions. She had always thought the little cat's behavior was cute and harmless. Now, however, with the playroom becoming a nursery, Miss Kitty's climbing and clawing posed a threat to the new baby.

"We're going to be one big happy family," Melanie announced as she got to her feet. "By the way, Mom, don't you think the crib would look great over there?"

Mrs. Parker was watching Miss Kitty playfully knocking things around on the dresser top.

"Mom, did you hear me?"

"Uh, yes," replied Melanie's mom staring at the impish cat pawing one of Melanie's hair ribbons. "We're going to be one big happy family."

Three

JUST as her mother had predicted, Melanie turned out to be a super interior decorator. As Mrs. Parker neared her due date, the messy playroom was almost magically transformed into a cheerful nursery.

A new coat of paint worked wonders for the room. Mr. Parker was in charge of the paint detail. Melanie and Miss Kitty helped. Of course they sloshed more paint on themselves than on the walls, but Mr. Parker didn't mind. He liked working on projects with his daughter. He didn't even get upset when Miss Kitty stepped in the paint tray and left paw prints all over the floor. He and Melanie actually giggled as they cleaned up after Miss Kitty.

When Melanie and Mrs. Parker went to buy new curtains, Melanie insisted on pink ones with pictures of playful little cats on them. "My little sister will love these," Melanie told the saleslady.

As days melted into weeks, the nursery became the focal point of attention for everyone in the Parker household. Each passing weekend brought a new and exciting addition to the room. The first bit of baby furniture the Parkers bought was a beautiful white bassinet.

"Isn't it wonderful, Melanie said to Miss Kitty as they peered into the bassinet. Melanie stood beside the bassinet. Miss Kitty was perched on top of it. "Our baby sister will sleep in here when she comes home from the hospital."

Melanie smoothed her hand across the mattress part of the bassinet. It felt soft and cool. "I still can't believe this is really happening," Melanie said softly. "When I was just a kid I used to dream about having a little sister. I wanted one so much. I used to be lonely lots of times." Melanie looked up at Miss Kitty. Miss Kitty stared back as if she understood.

Melanie lifted Miss Kitty off of the bassinet. "Then Mom and Dad got you for me." She stroked Miss Kitty's soft, white fur. "And I forgot all about a baby sister." Melanie cuddled Miss Kitty close to her. Miss Kitty snuggled right up and began to purr.

Melanie walked over to the couch and sat down. She looked around as she petted her cat. The room was really beginning to look like a nursery.

"Now I'll have you and a real baby sister," Melanie said. "It's almost too good to be true."

Just then Mr. Parker came in. He looked at his daughter and smiled. "What's this?" he teased. "Is our interior decorator goofing off? I'm glad I'm not paying you by the hour."

Melanie stood up. "Miss Kitty and I were just talking about how the room is shaping up."

Mr. Parker nodded in agreement. He walked over to his daughter and put an arm around her shoulders. "You're doing a super job. Once we get the rest of the old furniture out and the new stuff in, this will be a first class nursery."

"When will that be, Dad?"

"Soon," Mr. Parker replied. "You can't rush these things. We'll get done little by little."

Just as Mr. Parker had predicted, the job of redoing the playroom neared completion one step at a time. Huge nursery rhyme figures of Humpty Dumpty, Simple Simon, and others were hung on the freshly painted walls.

The musty old closet got a special facelift. Mr. Parker, with a little help from Melanie, built shelves and little compartments into the closet. Then Melanie and her mother stocked the shelves with diapers, blankets, powder, and other baby items. Miss Kitty even managed to get in on the act. She climbed in and out of the shelves and compartments until Mrs. Parker shooed her away.

Bit by bit the old playroom furniture began to

disappear. The bureau Miss Kitty used to climb on was replaced by an infant's dressing table. Of course, Melanie and Miss Kitty had to test it out.

"Now, keep still and pretend you're my new baby sister," Melanie told Miss Kitty as she carried her to the dressing stand.

Melanie placed Miss Kitty on the stand. She carefully unwrapped the blanket folded around her pet. "I want to practice," Melanie said as she took out powder and a diaper. "Mom might ask me to change the baby someday."

Miss Kitty didn't seem to like the sound of that. She began to wiggle and squirm. The powder fell out of Melanie's hand and sprinkled everywhere. A white cloud of dust covered Miss Kitty.

Miss Kitty's nose twitched. It wiggled. The sneezing fit that followed was so funny it made Melanie laugh out loud.

"Miss Kitty you're such a nut," Melanie said as she picked up her cat. "I guess I'll just have to practice after Mom has the baby." She pressed the powdery cat to her cheek. "I can hardly wait now that the nursery is almost ready."

Only two more things had to be done to finish the nursery. Melanie's old battered toy chest was moved to the attic. Miss Kitty's favorite, well-clawed chair was taken to the basement. The replacement for the couch was a brand new crib Melanie had helped pick out.

With all the new furniture in place, Mr. and Mrs. Parker considered the job done. In fact, they were very pleased with the outcome. On the Saturday they finished, they stood in the middle of the nursery and admired their work.

"It looks great," said Mr. Parker.

"Oh, George, I'm so happy," sighed Mrs. Parker with a smile.

"Melanie, we couldn't have done it without you," Mr. Parker said, winking at his daughter. Melanie wrapped her arms around her parents and hugged them tightly. She loved the nursery, but it needed one more little thing to make it perfect.

☆ ☆ ☆ ☆ ☆

At last, one day after school Melanie added the final touch to the baby's room. It was a crib mobile she had bought with her own money. Sandy Morgan, Melanie's babysitter, had helped her pick out a mobile that was safe and attractive. The mobile was a big secret. Melanie's parents knew nothing about it.

"There," said Melanie as she fastened the base of the mobile to the crib. "Isn't it neat?" Melanie looked at Miss Kitty. Miss Kitty was eyeing the mobile above the crib. The top of the mobile looked like the top of a circus tent. Dangling from the tent top were clowns and circus animals.

"I think it looks wonderful!" Melanie said to Miss Kitty. "Wait until Mom sees it. She'll be so surprised."

Miss Kitty made no reply. She just sat on the floor staring at the mobile, watching the clowns and animals sway from side to side.

"I can't wait any longer. I have to show it to

Mom." Melanie walked out of the nursery to find her mother.

"Hurry up, Mom," urged Melanie as she headed back to the baby's room. "Wait until you see what I bought for the baby. It's a surprise."

When Mrs. Parker walked into the nursery, she was more shocked than surprised. Running around the crib, clawing at the colorful moving objects of the mobile, was Miss Kitty.

"Miss Kitty! What are you doing?" yelled Melanie. Mrs. Parker was too stunned to talk. Her eyes widened in surprise, and her mouth dropped open.

Miss Kitty paid no attention to Melanie or Mrs. Parker. The cat scrambled around the crib. Miss Kitty jumped at the mobile and swatted the figures dangling overhead. She appeared to be having great fun and didn't seem to want to stop.

Finally Mrs. Parker regained the use of her tongue. "Melanie! Get that cat out of there!" she shouted angrily.

Instantly, Melanie obeyed. She reached in and

cornered Miss Kitty. The cat calmed down enough for Melanie to lift her out. "Bad cat! You almost broke my present." Melanie shook a finger at Miss Kitty in a threatening fashion. "Look at the mobile. It's all tangled up."

Mrs. Parker regained her composure. She didn't want Melanie to know how upset she was. "I'll fix it, honey," Mrs. Parker told Melanie. "The mobile is a wonderful surprise."

"I bought it with my own money," Melanie said.

"I'm sure the baby will love it. I do." Mrs. Parker looked at her daughter. Then she glanced at the cat in Melanie's arms. Miss Kitty calmly yawned as if to say, what did I do?

Mrs. Parker kissed Melanie on the forehead. "Thanks for the wonderful surprise," she said. "You take Miss Kitty outside. I'll straighten up in here. The mobile is wonderful. Thank you, sweetheart."

Melanie smiled broadly as she picked up Miss Kitty and headed outside.

Four

LATER that week the Parker family had an important meeting. Melanie's mom and dad sat together on the sofa. Melanie and Miss Kitty sat in the easy chair.

"This must be really important," Melanie said as she stroked Miss Kitty's back. "Dad came home from work early on a Friday, and he's not even going bowling."

"It is very important," acknowledged Melanie's mother. "And it's very serious."

"Gee, what's going on?" asked Melanie. "Is . . . everything all right?" Melanie looked at her mother's stomach. Now that her mom was visibly larger, Melanie had become more and more concerned about accidents. She teased her mom about fitting through doorways, but down deep Melanie was a worrywart. "The baby is okay, isn't it?" Melanie asked.

"Don't worry, sweetheart, the baby is fine," her father assured her. "Mom's last checkup was perfect."

Melanie was relieved, but more puzzled and concerned than ever. "Then what is this meeting all about?" asked Melanie. "It can't be my grades. School is almost out, and I know I'm getting promoted."

"It's Miss Kitty," Mrs. Parker said.

"Huh? What?" Melanie stared at her mother. Then she shot a glance at her father. Protectively, she picked up Miss Kitty and held her tightly. "What about Miss Kitty?" Melanie asked.

"Remember what happened in the crib the other day?" asked Mrs. Parker.

Melanie nodded. "Miss Kitty went after the mobile. Is that what this is about?"

"Yes, it is," said her father. "For some time now your mother and I have been worrying about

Miss Kitty. We're concerned about how she'll react to having a baby in the house."

"Miss Kitty loves little kids," Melanie insisted. "The thing in the crib was . . . an accident."

"With a baby," explained Mrs. Parker, "one little accident could be a big problem."

Melanie's dad nodded. "The baby could have been seriously injured if it had been in the crib when Miss Kitty went after the mobile," Melanie's father said.

Melanie sensed real trouble brewing. Her face started to get red. She knew her parents could see that she was becoming upset. "That's not fair," Melanie argued. "Just because Miss Kitty made one little mistake you're picking on her."

"That's not true, Melanie," said her father. "I don't think you're being very fair. We have to set priorities here. After all, who is more important, the new baby or Miss Kitty?"

Tears began to appear in the corners of Melanie's eyes. Her lips turned into a stern expression. She didn't answer right away.

Melanie's hesitance upset her father. His eyebrows began to twitch. They looked like they might jump off of his forehead. "Melanie? Melanie Parker! Answer me!" he demanded.

"George," scolded Mrs. Parker. "You're being too rough on Melanie. This is difficult enough."

Melanie jumped up. "You want to know who's more important? Okay. I'll tell you," she snapped in a defiant tone that was unlike her. "Miss Kitty is more important! She's a member of our family, too. And she was here first."

George Parker struggled to control his temper. He seldom yelled at his daughter, but this time was an exception. With his wife's due date so near, his nerves were on edge. "Miss Kitty is more important to you?" he shouted. "Well, young lady, for your information, Miss Kitty is going away before the baby arrives."

"What do you mean?" screamed Melanie. She stiffened in her chair. Never before had she ever talked back to her parents in that way. But it was like someone had roused a tiger deep inside her that she couldn't control.

"Please. Calm down everyone," begged Mrs. Parker. Mr. Parker sighed and wiped his eyebrows with his fingertips. Melanie turned away from her parents and sniffled. "This is supposed to be a family meeting," Mrs. Parker reminded them, "not All-Star pro wrestling. Can we try to respect each other's feelings and stop the yelling?"

Mr. Parker took a deep breath. He felt a bit ashamed of himself. Slowly he turned to face his daughter. "I'm sorry, Mel," her dad apologized. "I blew my cool."

Melanie wiped her watery eyes and faced her father. "I'm sorry, too," Melanie said. "But what did you mean when you said Miss Kitty is going away?"

"If we'll all sit down," said Mrs. Parker, "I'll explain."

Melanie dropped back into her chair. Her face was beet red. Her eyes were glazed. Nervously her foot twitched back and forth. Miss Kitty on the other hand didn't seem the least bit upset. She kept nuzzling Melanie's arm playfully.

When Mr. Parker was once again seated beside his wife, Mrs. Parker continued. "Melanie, for the baby's security and our own peace of mind, we've arranged for Miss Kitty to live on Uncle Bill's farm."

"NO! You can't be serious," yelled Melanie. This time the tears really started to flow. Big drops squeezed out of her eyes and wiggled down her rosy cheeks.

"Miss Kitty will be happy there," Melanie's mother told her. "You know Uncle Bill and Aunt Judy will take good care of her. They love animals."

"I'll take good care of her right here," argued Melanie. "Miss Kitty is mine. She's my cat. Why are you doing this to me?"

"We've explained why," replied Mr. Parker. "We don't want to do this, but we have to. Someday you'll understand."

Mrs. Parker continued. "On Saturday morning

we're driving Miss Kitty to Bill and Judy's farm."

"Saturday? That's tomorrow," Melanie sobbed.

"We thought it was best not to put it off any longer," explained Mr. Parker.

Mrs. Parker walked over to Melanie. She put an arm around her daughter. "We know how you feel, how hurt you are," she said in a soothing tone. "But honey, this isn't easy for us either."

Melanie jerked away from her mother's touch. "You! You! What about me?" she cried. "You don't care about me. All you care about is that crummy new baby."

Melanie got up. Her whole body was tembling in anger. Her parents were shocked and concerned. They never expected such a traumatic reaction. They didn't know what to do or say.

"I hate you," screamed Melanie. "I hate you both! I'll never forgive you for this. Never!" Cradling Miss Kitty in her arms, Melanie ran out of the room and out of the house.

"Don't, Sam," George Parker said as his wife started for the back door. "Let her go. Melanie

40

needs to be alone right now. She needs time to come to her senses."

Blinded by tears, Melanie made a mad dash through the house. She headed for the back part of the yard as the kitchen door slammed behind her. Holding Miss Kitty to her chest, she ran under her favorite tree and slumped down. Suddenly, all her pent-up emotions spilled out. Tears poured from her eyes, and she sobbed miserably.

"All these years I thought they cared about me," Melanie cried as she stroked Miss Kitty's fur. "They didn't. When I was lonely and wanted a baby sister, they were too busy to have one." She scratched behind Miss Kitty's pointed ears. "Now I have to give up what I love because they're finally ready to have another kid." Melanie covered her eyes with her hand and sobbed loudly. "It's not fair!" The tears flowed and kept coming.

"Want to talk?" asked a familiar voice.

Melanie wiped her eyes and looked up. Sandy Morgan took off her gardening gloves and sat down. "I'll go away if you want," Sandy said.

Melanie let Miss Kitty go and threw her arms around Sandy. "They're making me get rid of Miss Kitty," she sobbed. "I hate them!"

"Your parents?" Sandy asked.

Melanie nodded. "They're taking Miss Kitty to my aunt and uncle's farm tomorrow."

Sandy lifted Melanie's chin with her hand. She looked at her young friend's tear-stained face.

"Sometimes it's hard to understand why parents do things," Sandy said to Melanie.

"I won't let them take Miss Kitty." Melanie sobbed. "We'll run away!"

Sandy hugged Melanie. "That won't solve anything. Besides, running away is stupid." Sandy looked into Melanie's eyes. "You've always been tough, Mel. Remember when you fell off your bike and skinned your knees and elbows?"

Melanie straightened a bit. "I didn't cry

because that wimp Tommy Watson was watching," Melanie said.

"This is kind of the same thing," Sandy said. "You have to be tough. You have to pretend Tommy Watson is watching. Can you do that?"

Melanie nodded. "I guess so," she said. Sandy smiled. Melanie wiped away a tear with her arm. She sniffed and lifted her chin. "I'm okay now."

"Are you sure?" Sandy asked.

"Yeah! I'm just great!" She lied.

Sandy rose to her feet. "You can always talk to me, Mel, because we're friends." Sandy started to walk away. She stopped, paused, and looked back. "Remember Tommy Watson," she called. Then Sandy walked back to her garden.

Melanie leaned back against the tree trunk and looked at Miss Kitty. The little cat was chasing a bug in the grass. Even though she was still upset, Melanie had to smile. "Oh, Miss Kitty," she said reaching for her pet, "you always know how to make me feel better. What am I going to do without you?"

Five

EARLY the next morning, the Parkers prepared for the trip to Uncle Bill and Aunt Judy's farm. Melanie had spent the entire night sobbing and crying. And for the first time ever she'd locked her parents out of her room. Mr. and Mrs. Parker were so concerned they almost reconsidered taking Miss Kitty away. But they were convinced it was the right thing to do. They went ahead according to plan.

At breakfast, Melanie didn't eat a bite. She just stared blankly across the table at her folks. She only perked up a bit when her mother told her she could have a can of tuna from the cupboard for Miss Kitty.

"At least your last meal here is a good one,"

she whispered to Miss Kitty as she forked the tuna into the cat's dish. Miss Kitty began to gobble up the tasty flakes of fish. She ate hungrily. Tuna was her favorite. She didn't seem to have a care in the world.

Watching Miss Kitty eat made Melanie feel like crying, but she held it back. She didn't want her parents to see her do any more bawling. It was a matter of pride. She kept thinking about what Sandy had said. She kept thinking about that nerd Tommy Watson. Every time she thought about Tommy Watson, her tears dried up in her eyes.

"It's almost time to go," Mr. Parker said to Melanie as Miss Kitty continued to eat. "When Miss Kitty is done, wash out her dish and put it in a bag with her other things."

Melanie didn't answer. She just stared blankly at her father until he shrugged his shoulders and walked away. Melanie waited until Miss Kitty finished. Then she picked up Miss Kitty in one hand and the dish in the other.

Miss Kitty watched as Melanie rinsed the bowl in the sink and slipped it into a bag. Before she left the kitchen, Melanie went to the cupboard. She sneaked another can of tuna and placed it in Miss Kitty's bag. That taken care of, she began to pack the rest of Miss Kitty's things—her regular food, toys, and grooming articles.

Mrs. Parker walked in just as Melanie finished. "All done?" she asked. Melanie nodded, expressionlessly. "Your dad wanted to put Miss Kitty in a cardboard box for the trip," she continued.

Instantly, anger flashed on Melanie's face. Her facial features hardened into a scowl.

"But I told him you could hold Miss Kitty still during the drive," Mrs. Parker added. "You can, can't you?"

Melanie picked up Miss Kitty and held her tight. "You don't have to worry about us," she said. And as her mother walked away she added, " . . . ever again."

Melanie carried Miss Kitty and the bag out to

the car. She didn't say a word as she passed her mother and father at the front door.

"You'd think we were going to a funeral," grumbled Mr. Parker.

Mrs. Parker closed the front door and locked it. "Melanie is certainly treating us like we're not alive," she said to her husband.

"I just hope she snaps out of it soon," George Parker replied as he and his wife walked down the front steps. "I can hardly bear to watch her suffer so."

"Melanie won't even let herself cry," Mrs. Parker said. "And she's shutting us out completely."

George Parker nodded. "This is going to be one heck of a long drive."

When the Parkers reached the car, Melanie was already in the backseat with Miss Kitty. Mr. and Mrs. Parker got into the front and buckled their seat belts. Melanie's father turned the ignition key. The motor started, and he slipped the car into drive.

As they started down the driveway, Melanie

almost burst into tears. She looked at Miss Kitty. The little cat was cuddled in her lap, cozy and snug. A lump formed in Melanie's throat. One thing kept her from going into hysteria. "Tommy Watson," she muttered quietly to herself. "Tommy Watson! Tommy Watson!"

Miss Kitty didn't seem to know what was going on, or care for that matter. She slept quietly on Melanie's lap.

Some drives seem short. Others seem to drag on. The trip to the farm seemed to take an eternity. It was uncomfortably quiet all the way. Once Mrs. Parker tried to strike up a conversation about the beautiful rolling country-side. Melanie kind of grunted in reply.

Mr. Parker tried to make up a joke about some cows they passed along the roadside. Melanie didn't laugh. She didn't even smile. During the entire trip, the only noise in the backseat was an occasional meow from Miss Kitty, who seemed to take the tense journey in stride.

Around midday Mr. Parker turned onto the

dirt lane that led to Bill and Judy's dairy farm. "We're here," he announced, "finally."

"Thank goodness," sighed Mrs. Parker.

Melanie had no comment. She just kept Miss Kitty very close at hand. "Tommy Watson. . . Tommy Watson," she repeated quietly as her eyes watered.

When the car stopped, Aunt Judy and Uncle Bill came rushing out of the big, white farm house. "Well, it's about time," called Uncle Bill as Melanie's mom and dad got out of the car. "What did you do, get lost?"

"Stop teasing, Bill," Aunt Judy said as she hugged her sister. "How are you feeling now that your due date is almost here, Sam?"

"Oh, I'm feeling pretty well," Melanie's mother told Aunt Judy.

Uncle Bill and Mr. Parker shook hands. "How was the drive up, George?" Uncle Bill asked.

Melanie's dad arched his aching back. "It was long and tiring as usual," he replied. He leaned over to whisper to Uncle Bill. "The truth is, Bill, it was rotten. Melanie didn't say a word the entire trip."

"Speaking of Melanie," Uncle Bill yelled loudly. "Where is that cute niece of mine? Hiding in the car?"

Uncle Bill opened the back door of the car. "What do you need, an ingraved invitation?" Uncle Bill asked. "Come on out, and bring Miss Kitty with you. Breathe in some of this good, fresh country air."

Melanie forced a weak smile in reply. She exited the backseat and kissed her uncle and aunt hello. Usually Melanie was very excited about visiting the farm. It was one of her favorite places. But this time the farm had all the appeal of a jail. Melanie wished she were someplace else, anyplace else.

Miss Kitty, however, perked right up at the sight. Excitedly, she struggled to free herself from Melanie's grasp. The little cat became so hard to hold that Melanie dropped her. Off Miss Kitty shot like a furry bullet.

"Miss Kitty! Miss Kitty!" shrieked Melanie in terror. "Stop. Come back!"

"Whoa! Easy freckle face," said Aunt Judy as she gently put a hand on Melanie's shoulder. Aunt Judy always called Melanie freckle face. "Miss Kitty will be all right."

"She'll get lost," Melanie cried as she started after her quickly disappearing cat.

"She won't get lost, sweetheart," called Uncle Bill. "She's just exploring her new home."

Melanie paid no attention to Uncle Bill or anyone else. She raced after Miss Kitty. She ran faster than she did the time that bully, Brenda LaRue, had chased her to the bus.

"Don't worry about Melanie," Aunt Judy said to her sister. "She can't get hurt. Come inside. I have a great lunch prepared."

"It's a country style lunch," Uncle Bill added, winking.

Mr. Parker started for the farm house. Mrs. Parker lingered behind and looked toward the barn. Aunt Judy put her arm around her sister once again. "She'll be okay, Sam."

"You don't know how hard Melanie is taking this, Judy."

"You can tell me all about it over lunch," Aunt Judy told her sister. "You look tired. Come in and sit down."

Mrs. Parker smiled weakly. "Okay."

Melanie was frantic as she searched for Miss Kitty. She looked in and around the barn but couldn't find her pet. She called and called but Miss Kitty didn't come. Where is she? Melanie wondered. Where did she go? Melanie was haunted by all kinds of terrible worries.

Frustrated, tired, and depressed, Melanie flopped down on a bale of hay in the barn. She covered her face with her hands but refused to let herself cry. She didn't want her feelings to show. She just kept thinking about her conversation with Sandy. Dropping her hands to her sides, she exhaled deeply and loudly.

"Things are that bad, are they?" someone called.

Melanie looked up. Standing in the open barn doorway was Aunt Judy.

"I brought you a plate of fried chicken and potato salad," Aunt Judy said, "and some lemonade, too."

Aunt Judy walked over and handed the plate and glass to Melanie. "Thank you, Aunt Judy," said Melanie. "But I'm really not hungry."

Melanie's aunt set the dish and glass on the hay bale.

"You must be hungry, freckle face," said Aunt Judy. "Your mom told me you didn't eat a bite of breakfast, and I made lunch especially for you."

Melanie shrugged. "It smells good."

"Good?" questioned Aunt Judy, pretending to be shocked. "I thought my fried chicken and potato salad were the best in the U.S."

Melanie's lips showed a flicker of a smile. "I did say that once, didn't I?"

"You did," her aunt reminded her. "The last time you visited, you pigged out on chicken and potato salad."

"Well, maybe I'll try just a little," Melanie said, sipping some lemonade from the frosty glass. Melanie set the plate on her lap and began to nibble on a drumstick.

Aunt Judy sat down beside her. She glanced around. "Miss Kitty hasn't shown up yet?" she asked.

Melanie shook her head. She swallowed and dabbed the napkin against her lips. "You don't think anything happened to her, do you?"

"What could happen to a cat on a farm?" Aunt Judy answered. "She probably met Old Tom."

Melanie brightened. She'd forgotten all about Aunt Judy's pet tabby, Old Tom.

"You know," Aunt Judy continued, "we love you very much. We all love you very much. We're not doing this just to make you unhappy."

Melanie stopped a fork of potato salad in midair and looked at her aunt sternly. Then she shoved the food into her mouth.

"We'll take good care of Miss Kitty," Aunt Judy continued. "I promise. Miss Kitty will love it here. Uncle Bill even agreed to let her sleep in the house. We'll take special care of her for you. And she'll always be your cat. She'll just be living with us."

"I wish I could believe that," Melanie said before she drained her glass of lemonade.

"You can," Aunt Judy assured her.

"But where is she now?" A twinge of alarm sounded in Melanie's voice. "What if she doesn't come back before we have to leave?"

"Miss Kitty will probably be back any minute," Aunt Judy said as she got to her feet. "Now let's go into the house and get you some more lemonade."

Reluctantly, Melanie stood up and followed her aunt. She was thirsty. And she knew if she sat in the barn one minute more she would burst right into tears, Tommy Watson or not.

☆ ☆ ☆ ☆ ☆

Mr. Parker checked his watch as he sat on the front porch. "It's really getting late," he said to his wife. "We've got a long way to go."

Mrs. Parker looked at her husband. "That silly cat would pick now to run away. But we can't just go like this."

"I know," Mr. Parker responded, nodding.

The Parkers peered out at the farmyard. Melanie had hunted for Miss Kitty all afternoon. She'd started looking again right after supper, and she was still at it.

Aunt Judy walked up to the porch. She had been helping Melanie search. "I swear, I can't imagine where that cat got to," she said to the others.

"Miss Kitty will turn up, Jude," her husband assured her. "You know Old Tom. Sometimes he doesn't come home for two or three days."

Mr. Parker shook his head sadly. "We can't wait that long," he said. "We have to go now."

Mrs. Parker agreed. "I'll get my purse," she said. "I'd hoped Miss Kitty would be back by now."

"Melanie," called Mr. Parker. "Melanie! Come over here please. And bring Miss Kitty's bag from the car."

When Melanie heard her father call, her blood felt like it froze in her veins. She knew what he wanted. But she didn't believe he would make her leave now, would he? Melanie got Miss Kitty's bag from the car and took it to the porch. Aunt Judy came out of the house with Melanie's mother.

"Give Aunt Judy the bag, honey," Melanie's dad instructed.

Melanie looked from one adult to the other. Her eyes were red and filled with tears. Mr. Parker and the others fidgeted. "These are Miss Kitty's toys," muttered Melanie as she handed the bag to her aunt. "Her bowl is in there, too. There's also"—she paused—"a can of tuna for Miss Kitty's supper," she added.

Melanie looked at her mom.

Mrs. Parker tried to smile. "I knew you took the tuna," she said to her daughter. "It's okay."

Mr. Parker turned to Aunt Judy. "Thanks for the delicious lunch and supper," he said.

Uncle Bill got up and kissed Mrs. Parker on the cheek. Melanie tensed. She knew good-byes when she saw and heard them.

"Forget Tommy Watson," she said to herself as tears squirted from her eyes. "We can't go yet!" she yelled, so loudly that it surprised everyone on the porch.

Her father was startled by her outburst. His eyebrows began to dance a jig. "Melanie don't make a scene!"

"Calm down, George," Mrs. Parker said.

"It's okay," Uncle Bill said. "We understand how hard this is for Melanie." The adults started down the stairs.

"But we can't go yet! I won't go!" Melanie shrieked. She wrapped her arms around one of the front porch pillars and clung to it like an oppossum. "I'm not leaving until I see Miss Kitty. Miss Kitty! Here, Kitty, Kitty!" she screamed as tears poured out of her eyes and streamed down her face. "Here, Kitty! Here, Miss Kitty!"

The adults stopped dead in their tracks.

"George, can't we wait a little longer?" begged Mrs. Parker.

Mr. Parker's heart was in his throat. Seeing Melanie act like that both hurt and embarrassed him at the same time. "We have to go now!" he said firmly.

Mrs. Parker walked over to her daughter. Aunt Judy did, too. "Please let go of the porch pillar," Melanie's mom requested.

"Why don't you just leave me here with Miss Kitty," Melanie sobbed. "You'll have the new baby soon. Let me be Aunt Judy and Uncle Bill's kid. You don't want me anymore."

Aunt Judy eyed her sister in a concerned fashion. Then she went up to Melanie and put her arms around her. "If we ever have a child," Aunt Judy said, "we'd like her to be just like you.

But you know and we know you can't stay here. You have to go home, Melanie. Now please let go."

Melanie regained a bit of composure. She let loose of the pillar and tried to stop crying. What's the use? I can't win, she thought. Melanie started down the porch steps. She paused to give her aunt and uncle a farewell kiss. Then she opened the door to the car. Still sobbing, she climbed into the backseat.

"That was terrible," Mr. Parker said to his relatives. "I feel awful about this."

"We all do," Uncle Bill said as his head drooped sadly.

The women hugged one last time and walked to the car. The Parkers got in. "Keep in close touch now," Aunt Judy said. Then she looked in the back where Melanie was brooding. "I'll phone you as soon as we find Miss Kitty. I promise, freckle face. Don't worry."

Melanie didn't even look at her aunt. Why don't you all leave me alone, she thought.

With final good-byes said, Mr. Parker put the

car in gear. As he made a full circle in the drive, he passed the barn.

It was just then that Miss Kitty returned. As the car sped away Miss Kitty madly raced after it.

"Look!" cried Aunt Judy pointing at the cat as it chased the car down the lane. "It's Miss Kitty. Get her Bill!" Uncle Bill ran after Miss Kitty.

In the car the Parkers didn't notice what was going on behind them. They were all too deep in thought. Melanie was thinking about the new baby and how much she hated it. The new baby was the cause of all her troubles.

As the Parkers turned onto the highway, Miss Kitty hesitated. She slowed down just enough that Uncle Bill caught up to her. He picked the cat up and gently cradled her in his huge arms. "Relax, Miss Kitty," he whispered. "We're going to take good care of you. Let's head back to the house for a saucer of fresh milk. This is your new home now."

Six

MELANIE couldn't get over the incident at Aunt Judy's farm. Nothing anyone said or did changed her attitude. Day after day she just seemed to go through the motions of living. She never laughed or smiled. She couldn't break out of her depression, because she didn't want to.

Even when Aunt Judy phoned with the good news about finding Miss Kitty, Melanie didn't snap out of it. Melanie was trying to shut herself off from everyone and everything.

Melanie's parents were so busy planning for the arrival of the new baby that Melanie felt they were ignoring her. But that suited Melanie just fine. She went to school. She came home. She watched TV or listened to music in her room. She didn't much care about the new baby. The only thing she cared about had been snatched away from her. She knew Miss Kitty was gone for good. She couldn't pretend otherwise.

During those bad days, Melanie spent a lot of time sitting under her favorite tree in the backyard. One afternoon Sandy Morgan walked over to chat.

"I heard my Tommy Watson advice didn't work out," Sandy said as she sat on the soft grass. "Your mom told mine. What happened at the farm?"

"It worked for a while," Melanie answered. "Then it kind of struck out."

"Well, having to leave without seeing Miss Kitty was no piece of cake. It took real guts."

"Yeah," grunted Melanie as she lay back against the tree trunk, "some guts. You should have seen me hanging onto that pillar screaming."

"Anyway, you must be excited now that your

mom's due date is almost here." Sandy waited for an answer.

Melanie stuck a long sliver of grass in her mouth and clenched her teeth.

"Aren't you excited?" Sandy asked.

"Who cares?" Melanie asked as she rolled onto her stomach. "Who cares about the little brat? As soon as I'm old enough I'm getting out of here. Then the brat can have the nursery and my room, too."

"I thought you decided running away didn't make any sense?"

"That was before," Melanie answered. "During our last talk the Tommy Watson advice seemed like a good idea, too." Melanie got up and started to walk toward the house. "I have to go in now. I have lots to do. You know how it is, this being the last week of school and all."

Melanie left Sandy standing there. She knew it was rude, but she didn't care. She didn't much feel like being nice or polite to anyone, and that included Sandy.

☆　☆　☆　☆　☆

That night Melanie had trouble sleeping. When her dad rushed into her room at three in the morning, she was already half awake. He flicked on the light and began to babble nervously. "Wake up! Wake up, Mel! It's time! It's time!" he said nervously.

Melanie sat up slowly and rubbed her eyes. "W-What's going on?" she muttered.

"T-The baby," stammered Mr. Parker.

The first thing Melanie noticed was her dad's eyebrows. They were twitching up a storm.

"Grab your things," Melanie's father said. "You'll go next door to the Morgans like we arranged."

Mr. Parker went back out into the hallway. "Samantha," he called, "is everything okay? Should I phone the doctor?"

"I'm fine, George. There's plenty of time," Mrs. Parker assured him. "I've already phoned Doctor Kates. Is Melanie up?"

"Huh?" called George as he bumped into the table in the hall. The phone went clunking to the floor. "Mel's up," he yelled. "Where's your suitcase?"

Melanie climbed out of bed sleepily. She yawned and went to the closet to get the overnight bag she'd packed weeks ago. She slipped on her robe and went out into the hall.

Her father was turning out the pockets of his pants looking for something. "The keys," he sputtered. "I can't find the car keys!"

Mrs. Parker came out of the bedroom with her suitcase in hand. "George, I have the keys and the suitcase. Let's go." She gasped, and touched one hand to her stomach. She took a deep breath, then added, "We'd better hurry."

George Parker sprang to his wife's side. He carefully ushered her down the stairs as Melanie followed. The Parkers rushed out the front door and locked it behind them. Mrs. Parker stopped near the car for another deep breath. She stood silently for a minute then looked at Melanie.

"The Morgans are expecting you," Mrs. Parker said with a smile. Then she kissed Melanie on the forehead. "I'll phone you from the hospital. Wish me luck." She took her daughter's hand in her own and gently squeezed it.

Melanie's ironclad resistence melted. At that moment Melanie had never felt closer to her mom. Melanie threw her arms around her mother and gave her a giant bear hug. "Good luck, Mom. I love you," she whispered.

"Go on over to the Morgans now," said Mr. Parker to Melanie as he put his wife's suitcase in the car. He opened the door for his wife, and Mrs. Parker got in.

As Melanie walked next door, Mr. Parker backed the car out of the driveway. He waited at the end of the drive for the Morgans' front porch light to come on.

Sandy Morgan opened the front door of her house as Melanie approached. Melanie waved as her parents drove off down the dark street. When the car was out of sight she looked up at Sandy.

"Come in, Melanie," said Mr. Morgan. "You can bunk with Sandy. The spare bed is all ready."

"Thank you, Mr. Morgan." Melanie went in. Slowly she and Sandy began to climb the stairs to the bedroom. Melanie paused at the top of the stairs. "Sandy," she said, "I'm sorry about what I said in the backyard yesterday."

Sandy's tired face brightened. "Forget it," Sandy said, giving Melanie a hug.

The two girls started for the bedroom. "You know," Melanie continued, "this baby thing just might work out after all." She smiled and winked at Sandy.

"I know," Sandy said as she opened the door to her room. "What do you think it's going to be, a boy or a girl?"

"Are you kidding," answered Melanie as she went in. "It's going to be a girl. For sure!"

After breakfast the next morning, a weary Mr. Parker showed up at the Morgan house. "George, you look awful," said Mrs. Morgan as she opened the front door. "Can I get you some coffee?"

"Thanks, I can use it," Mr. Parker answered. He walked in. "Where is everyone?"

"Mike left early for work," Mrs. Morgan said as she started for the kitchen.

"That husband of yours works too hard."

"Don't I know it. How is Samantha?"

"She and the baby are doing great!" Mr. Parker answered, sounding like a cartoon tiger during a breakfast cereal commercial. "Where are the girls?"

"Sandy is at school," Mrs. Morgan called from the kitchen. "I let Melanie stay home like you instructed. She's in the den watching cartoons." George Parker headed for the den to tell his daughter the news.

"Hello, big sister," he called as he stepped into the den. "Good news. Everyone is fine. Mom sends her love."

As soon as Melanie spotted her dad, she launched herself from the sofa and rocketed into his arms. Instantly she began to chatter happily. "What's my sister like? Is she cute? Does she have freckles? Does she look like me?"

"Whoa, slow down," Mr. Parker said. "The truth is the baby looks like me," he announced proudly.

"Yuck!" teased Melanie as she began to smile. "What looks to wish on a baby girl."

"Who said it was a girl?" Mr. Parker answered. "Baby Matthew looks just like his old man." Mr. Parker beamed proudly.

The words stung Melanie as sharply as a slap in the face. She stepped back from her father in a daze. "B-Baby Matthew?" she sputtered. "You mean I have a brother? It's a boy?"

"A boy!" shouted Mrs. Morgan as she entered holding Mr. Parker's cup of coffee. "How wonderful! Congratulations, George!"

Melanie's father was shining with joy.

"But I don't want a brother!" snapped Melanie.

"I want a sister. I gave up Miss Kitty . . . for a crummy brother?"

"Melanie," her father gasped. "Don't talk like that." He raised an eyebrow and glared at his daughter.

"The brat will probably grow up to be a wimp like Tommy Watson," Melanie continued as she backed away from her father. "All this for a brother!"

George Parker stepped toward his daughter. "Come on, Mel, let's go home," he said. He reached out and put his hands on her shoulders. "You're tired," he told her. "You've had it very tough these last few weeks."

"You'll feel differently when you see your new brother," Mrs. Morgan said to Melanie. "I know you were counting on having a sister. But just give your brother a chance, sweetheart!"

Melanie tensed. She felt disappointed and cheated. She wasn't sure she'd ever feel differently about having a brother.

Seven

THE day the baby came home was a big day for everyone except Melanie. It felt more like doomsday to her. She didn't even want to be around her little brother.

Mr. Parker handed out chocolate cigars that said "It's a boy!" to everyone in sight. All of the Parkers' friends "oohed" and "ahhed" over little Matthew. Even Sandy, Melanie's old standby pal, fawned over the little kid. Melanie thought the whole scene was corny and disgusting.

"Isn't Matthew cute?" Sandy asked as she plopped down on the sofa in the Parkers' living room. Melanie was next to her in the easy chair.

"Yeah, sure," Melanie answered, "if you think

shriveled up beets are cute."

Sandy frowned at Melanie.

"Well, that's what he looks like to me," Melanie muttered. "I never saw anyone that color in my life."

"All newborn babies look like that," Sandy said in defense of Matthew.

"How would you know?"

Sandy ignored Melanie's nasty tone. "I learned about it in health class at school," Sandy answered. "In a couple weeks your brother won't be reddish and wrinkled anymore."

"Wow! Super! Are all babies baldies, too?" Melanie asked. "His head looks like a cue ball."

Melanie turned to eye the crowd of grown-ups clustered around the baby's bassinet. "It makes me sick to my stomach the way they fuss over that kid. It's been going on for hours."

"Are you jealous?" Sandy questioned.

"Of that bassinet bozo?" Melanie snapped. "Not hardly." She fidgeted in her chair.

"Well, you act like you are," Sandy said as she

helped herself to snacks on the coffee table. "And I still think your brother's cute."

Melanie crossed her legs. "Cute, huh? Then you can come over and help change his dirty diapers. You should see those things. ICK!"

Sandy smiled. "I don't have to worry about dirty diapers," teased Sandy. "That's your job, big sister."

"I'll never touch a diaper," Melanie swore. "If I do lightning can strike me."

Melanie's bolt of diaper lightning struck about six weeks later. Until then Melanie had managed to almost completely avoid helping her mother with little Matthew. Melanie used every excuse she could think of to stay away from her baby brother. Whenever her parents tried to force her to help, Melanie got moody and grumpy. Mr. and Mrs. Parker didn't push it. They hoped she would work out the problem on her own.

Melanie spent most of the first half of summer vacation moping around in front of the TV set. Some vacation, she thought. Because of her dumb baby brother, her family couldn't go away on vacation this year. Melanie felt like the world was against her.

"Melanie, turn down the volume on the TV," her mother called from the nursery. "It's too loud. I'm trying to put Matty down for his nap."

Melanie rose begrudgingly and adjusted the set. "Melanie do this. Melanie do that," she complained under her breath as she sat back down in front of the screen.

A commercial came on. It was one for cat food. The cat in the commercial was fluffy and white. Melanie thought it looked a lot like Miss Kitty. Of course, it wasn't Miss Kitty. But the resemblance was close enough to reopen old wounds. Melanie got a bit misty watching the cat in the ad. It reminded her of the way Miss Kitty used to bound happily around the playroom.

"Melanie, I need you," her mother called.

"Come to the nursery, please. And no excuses this time."

"Oh, all right," Melanie yelled back. "I'm coming. I'm coming." Melanie took her time going up to the nursery. After all that had happened, she hated that room with a passion.

"Melanie, will you hurry? I really need your help," her mother said.

Melanie could hear the baby crying. "Boy, that kid is noisy," she grumbled to herself. "I can't think of one thing I like about him. I'd trade him for Miss Kitty any day." The cat food commercial had really stirred up her emotions. She felt like a thundercloud about to erupt as she entered the baby's room.

Little Matthew was lying in the crib spouting tears like a fountain. His bottom was bare and Mrs. Parker was rubbing cream on his backside.

Melanie stared at her little brother. At least Sandy Morgan had been right about some things. Little Matthew was no longer red and wrinkled. In fact, his clear pink skin was almost perfect.

Even a few strands of blond hair had sprouted on his fuzzy head. The funny way he wiggled his fingers made Melanie smile in spite of herself.

"I'm out of diapers," Mrs. Parker told Melanie. "Look in the closet, way in the back. See if you can find some."

Melanie headed for the closet. "I'll have to tell your father to stop and buy more diapers on the way home from work," her mother added, rolling Matthew onto his back. She tickled the baby's tummy and uttered soothing sounds to try to calm him. It worked. Little Matt stopped crying.

Melanie opened the closet and poked around in the back. It was dark. As she fumbled around in the shadows, she found a box with a few extra diapers way in the far corner. "I get every dirty job there is around here," she grumbled as she started to back out.

Just then her hand touched something that felt out of place in the closet. Melanie jumped. It squeaked! The odd noise caught her off guard.

"What was that?" Mrs. Parker asked, glancing

across the room toward the closet.

Melanie looked closer at the strange object. It was a toy mouse. "It's Miss Kitty's favorite toy mouse," Melanie gasped. "So this is where it was." Melanie hadn't been able to find it when she packed Miss Kitty's things.

"Melanie, are you okay?" her mom asked. Melanie crawled out of the closet and stood up. In one hand were the diapers. In the other was Miss Kitty's toy mouse. Tears were cascading down Melanie's cheeks. She was so upset she was trembling. "Here are the crummy diapers," she sneered as she threw them on the floor near the crib. Clutching Miss Kitty's toy in her hand, Melanie ran out of the nursery in a huff.

Almost instantly Little Matthew began to cry again. "There, there," cooed Mrs. Parker as she lefted the baby from the crib. "It's all right. It's all right."

But deep inside Mrs. Parker knew everything wasn't all right. She wondered if things would ever be right again in the Parker house.

Eight

AT the end of July when work slowed on the dairy farm, Aunt Judy and Uncle Bill arrived for a visit. Before their truck came to a stop in the Parkers' driveway, Melanie shot out the front door.

"Hi, Aunt Judy! Hi, Uncle Bill!" Melanie shouted excitedly as she ran toward the pickup.

"Hi, freckle face," called Aunt Judy as she waved through the open window. "My, how you've grown."

Uncle Bill stepped out. "She sure has. How old are you now, seventeen? Eighteen?"

Melanie smiled at her uncle's joking. "You know my birthday is just around the corner," she answered. "I'll be ten."

"Really," replied Uncle Bill scratching his head as if amazed. "I could've sworn you were older." He winked at Melanie, and then he helped his wife out of the truck.

Melanie's dad strolled down the sidewalk to greet his relatives. "Hi, Judy." He kissed her on the cheek. "I saved some cigars for you and Bill," he said holding out several chocolate cigars.

Uncle Bill took them and read the wrapping. "It's a boy!" he shouted. He nudged his wife gently with his elbow. "I told you it would be a boy, didn't I?"

"I wish you'd have told me," Mr. Parker kidded. All three adults laughed.

"Come on in," Mr. Parker said, motioning them toward the house. "Samantha is upstairs dressing the baby. Wait until you see him. He's a big boy already."

"I wish we could have gotten away sooner," Aunt Judy said, apologetically.

"We understand," replied Mr. Parker.

As the group started toward the house, Melanie stepped into her aunt's path. "Aunt Judy, how is Miss Kitty?"

Aunt Judy stopped and smiled at her niece. Then she spoke to the men. "You guys go in. Tell Sam I'll be right up. You don't mind do you?"

"Of course not," Mr. Parker said as he and Uncle Bill headed for the house. Then he whispered to his brother-in-law, "This is the first time Melanie has smiled in weeks."

After the men went into the house, Melanie and Aunt Judy sat on the front step. "Is Miss Kitty happy on the farm?" Melanie asked.

"Is she ever," Aunt Judy said. "That little cat turned out to be the best mouse catcher we've ever had. And is she comical! Just two days ago she was in the barn and fell into a pail of milk. When she climbed out, she was the funniest sight I've ever seen."

Aunt Judy laughed at the thought. Melanie chuckled, too. "That's Miss Kitty all right," Melanie said.

Aunt Judy nodded. "In the evenings, Miss Kitty cuddles up on Uncle Bill's lap while he sits in his easy chair. Farm living is in that cat's blood. Miss Kitty is very happy."

Melanie was pleased and a bit hurt by the news of Miss Kitty. She wanted her pet to be happy in her new home, but not that happy. It didn't sound like Miss Kitty missed her at all. And Melanie missed Miss Kitty a lot.

Aunt Judy continued about Miss Kitty. "Old Tom and Miss Kitty are practically inseparable. You won't believe . . ."

Aunt Judy was interrupted by the opening of the front door. It was Melanie's mother. "Okay girls, break up this gossip session," she teased. "Come in and see the baby, Judy."

"I'll be right there, Sam," answered Aunt Judy. "Wow! You're looking great. Your figure is starting to come back already."

Aunt Judy stood up. She smiled at Melanie. "I'll finish the rest of the news later, freckle face." Aunt Judy walked over to her sister. They hugged and kissed. Then they walked into the house jabbering about the new baby.

Melanie sat on the front step even after the door closed. She didn't want to go in and hear all that gooshy stuff about whose eyes and nose little Matthew had. She'd rather think about Miss Kitty.

"A good mouser, huh?" she said to herself. "Mouse," she thought remembering what she'd found in the nursery closet a while back. I have to remember to give Miss Kitty's toy to Aunt Judy before she goes home.

Later everyone was relaxing after dinner in the Parker living room. Mrs. Parker had Matthew in her arms. Aunt Judy was admiring the sleeping tot. Uncle Bill was telling Melanie's dad that he expected a record corn crop this year.

When Melanie walked in, everyone's attention shifted to her.

"Hi, freckle face. Where have you been hiding since dinner?" Aunt Judy asked.

"I've been in the backyard," answered Melanie. She smiled.

"That's nice to see, sweetheart," Mrs. Parker said. "Smiles on your face have been few and far between lately."

"She's smiling because we're here," kidded Uncle Bill. "It's her sneaky way of telling us we have funny faces, Jude."

"That's not true," Melanie quickly replied as she sat on the carpet. "I mean it is and it isn't. I'm smiling because you're here. I wish you'd visit more often."

"That's hard to do, honey," Uncle Bill explained. "Being a farmer isn't a nine to five job. There is always something extra left to do."

"Maybe Melanie could come and visit us in August," suggested Aunt Judy. "She could stay for a week or two as sort of a vacation."

"I'd be glad to have her," Uncle Bill said. "I'll put her right to work."

Melanie gushed with excitement. Happiness bubbled out of every pore. She'd get a vacation after all and a chance to visit Miss Kitty, too. "YA-HOO! Can I Dad?" she yelled jumping up.

"Quiet, honey. You'll wake the baby," warned Mrs. Parker as she shifted Matthew to her other shoulder.

Mr. Parker stroked his chin thoughtfully. "I don't see why not," he said to Melanie. He noticed a bulge in the back of her jeans. "What's in your pocket?" he asked.

Melanie tapped her backside. "Oh, this?" She took a toy mouse out of her pocket. "This is Miss Kitty's," she said handing the toy to Aunt Judy. "It's Miss Kitty's favorite. I bought it for her when she was a kitten."

Aunt Judy took the mouse. "Kittens!" she said. She shook her finger in the air as if remembering something. "Kittens!" she repeated. "I started to tell Melanie about it when we arrived. Then I got so caught up in talking about the baby and dinner that I completely forgot."

"Forgot what?" asked Mrs. Parker.

"Stop beating around the bush," Uncle Bill told his wife. "Tell them the exciting news."

"Guess what, Melanie," said Aunt Judy. "Miss Kitty is going to have babies. She's going to have kittens."

Melanie tensed. Her whole body went rigid. Her smile slid down her face and turned into a scowl. "No!" she screamed. "Not Miss Kitty! All this trouble started with Mom having a baby."

Her shouts woke Little Matthew. He shook his tiny fists and began to howl. The adults were shocked at Melanie's remarks. They were frozen to their seats.

"I don't want to go to your dumb farm!" Melanie yelled at Aunt Judy. "Your farm ruined Miss Kitty. With new babies she'll ignore me, too! You can keep your stupid vacation!"

"Melanie!" George Parker jumped to his feet, eyebrows going up and down. "I've had about enough of your temper fits. This is one time you have to be punished. You go to your room right now! And don't come out! Do you understand, young lady?"

With a nasty look on her face, Melanie nodded. She turned and left. She ran up to her room, banging the stairs with her feet.

Mrs. Parker managed to calm Matthew, and the adults eased back in their seats.

"I don't know what I'm going to do with that girl," said Mr. Parker. "I've tried to be patient, but this has gone on for too long. What she needs is a good spanking."

"I think you're wrong, George," Aunt Judy argued. "Giving up Miss Kitty left a big gap in Melanie's life. She needs something to fill it."

"I agree," Mrs. Parker said. "And I can think of something to fill that gap."

"Me, too," Aunt Judy said.

"Me, three," Uncle Bill chimed in.

Mr. Parker looked at the others. They were all smiling smugly. "Why doesn't anyone tell me anything?" he grumbled.

"We plan to dear," said Mrs. Parker.

Nine

AFTER Uncle Bill and Aunt Judy left for home, Melanie stayed in a cranky mood. Every time she thought about her father punishing her, she nearly foamed at the mouth. Why does everything always seem to go wrong for me? she wondered.

Even the thought of her upcoming birthday didn't cheer her up. What difference will turning ten make? Things will still be the same, she thought. Everyone and everything will still be against me.

First it was her parents getting rid of Miss Kitty. Then Sandy thought her icky brother was cute. Last and worst of all, Miss Kitty had turned traitor. "Kittens," she grumbled. "They're as bad as brothers!"

Melanie threw herself on her bed. The record she was listening to was scratched, but she didn't even notice. For a few minutes she lay there deep in thought. The record hit a scratch and began to repeat the same words over and over again. Finally Melanie got up and shut off the record player. Her room was really quiet.

Just then Melanie heard an odd noise. It sounded like it came from the nursery. "Mom?" Melanie called. There was no answer. Melanie shrugged her shoulders. Then she heard the noise again. "I'd better check it out," she said to herself.

Melanie went into the hall. She turned toward the nursery. The noise was coming from there. "Mom," she said again, this time softly. The baby was supposed to be down for his afternoon nap.

When she received no answer, Melanie went to the nursery. Her little brother was wide awake. He was smiling and kicking excitedly. Matthew's heels striking against the mattress was the sound Melanie had heard.

Melanie looked at her brother lying there in the crib she had helped pick out. For the first time, she really saw him. A smile spread across her lips. "What are you doing, practicing to be an Olympic sprinter, Matty," she teased.

Melanie caught herself. "I called the kid, Matty," she mumbled to herself. "Am I going soft, or is this kid finally getting to me?"

Little Matthew squealed in delight. His feet and hands were thumping the crib mattress wildly. "What are you so excited about?" Melanie whispered, moving closer to her brother.

Then she noticed that his eyes were focused on the crib mobile over his head. "You really love that mobile, don't you," she said. Melanie jiggled it once or twice. She gently tapped Matthew's tummy with her fingertip. "Your big sister bought that for you with her own money."

Melanie stared at the baby. He was so tiny and helpless. Melanie felt guilty about all the rotten

things she'd said about him. "I guess all this really isn't your fault," she mumbled. "You didn't ask to be born." She looked at her brother and went to tickle him again.

Matthew's little hand touched hers. His tiny fingers closed around her fingers. "Wow, you're strong," said Melanie as Matthew tugged at her hand, then let it go. "I wish you could have met Miss Kitty. You guys would have been great pals."

Just then, Mrs. Parker came into the nursery. She stopped in the doorway shocked to see Melanie bending over the crib. "I thought I heard the baby," she said in a tone above a whisper.

Instantly Melanie took a step back. Her smile faded. "He's been up for a few minutes," Melanie replied. "I came in to make sure he was all right." Melanie turned and left the room.

"Don't go," said Mrs. Parker.

"I'm listening to records," Melanie said.

"Well, thanks for looking in on Matt," Mrs. Parker called as Melanie walked into her room and closed the door.

Mrs. Parker looked at Matthew. He was still gazing at the mobile. "Now what was that all about," she wondered out loud.

☆ ☆ ☆ ☆ ☆

After that day a gradual change came over Melanie. She stopped making excuses when her mom needed a hand with the baby. She didn't offer to help, but she was right there when her mom called.

Late one night, Mrs. Parker told Mr. Parker about the change. "You know, George, I think Melanie is finally starting to like her brother."

Mr. Parker looked at his wife. "I wish I could believe that," he sighed.

"It's true. During the day when you're at work, she's more help than she's ever been."

"Well, at least she doesn't call the baby 'the brat' anymore," agreed Mr. Parker. "That's some progress."

"I really mean it, George. I can't put my finger on it, but there's a change in Melanie."

"I don't want to sound like a mean father," said Mr. Parker, "but I'll believe it when I see it."

Ten

MELANIE'S outlook on life improved as her birthday approached. She was really looking forward to the big party her parents always had in her honor.

One afternoon in early August, Melanie was in her room working on the guest list when she heard her brother wail. It was different than any crying she'd ever heard before. His shrill cries seemed to pierce her ears. The noise made her shudder. "I thought he was sleeping," she said to herself.

Melanie jumped off her bed and looked down the hall. She saw her mom dash into the nursery. Melanie started back to her bed. Usually

Matthew stopped crying a few minutes after Mrs. Parker picked him up. But not this time. If anything, his crying got worse. It made Melanie a little nervous.

She walked down to the nursery and peeked in. Mrs. Parker was walking back and forth with Matthew in her arms. He was screaming at the top of his little lungs.

"What's wrong, Mom?"

"I don't know," Mrs. Parker replied in a slightly alarmed tone. "I really don't know. I can't get Matthew to stop crying."

Melanie went in. Tears gushed out of Matthew's eyes. He acted like he was in pain. Melanie grimaced.

"It could be colic. It could be gas. Or it could be something serious," Mrs. Parker said as she anxiously paced the floor with the baby in her arms. "Nothing I do seems to help. I wish your father were here. I'm a little worried."

"Do you want me to call him at work?" Melanie offered.

Mrs. Parker looked at Matthew's teary face. Then she glanced at Melanie. "No, but maybe I'd better call the doctor," she said. "I've never seen Matthew like this."

Melanie stepped toward her mother. "I'll watch him, Mom, while you call the doctor."

"Thanks, Melanie," Mrs. Parker said, laying Matthew in the crib. His crying increased. "Watch him carefully. I'll be right back." Mrs. Parker ran from the room as Melanie stepped toward the crib and tried to comfort her brother with soothing sounds.

Mrs. Parker dialed the doctor's number, but the line was busy. She tried again, but it was still busy. She nervously paced the floor, then lifted the phone from the hook to dial once more.

But suddenly she noticed the silence. Matthew wasn't crying anymore. Oh, no! What happened? she wondered. She quickly hung up the phone. She ran to the nursery expecting something awful.

Instead she found something wonderful. "Mel. . ." The words froze in her throat. Matthew was smiling and kicking and cooing. His blue eyes were glued to his big sister as she made funny faces at him from the edge of the crib.

"Look at this one, Matty," Melanie said as she opened her mouth wide and wiggled her tongue rapidly. Then she noticed her mother. "Hi, Mom. You don't have to worry. I guess it was just gas. Matt's fine now."

Mrs. Parker wiped a tear from her eye. "So I see," she said as she stepped into the room. "I think we're all fine now."

Melanie stepped back. "Want to pick him up?" she asked her mother.

Mrs. Parker nodded. She reached into the crib and lifted the contented infant out of his bed. "Here!" she said to Melanie. "You're the one with the magic touch. You hold him." Melanie's mother carefully handed baby Matthew to his sister.

Melanie smiled from ear to ear as she took her baby brother in her arms for the first time. As she hugged him she felt warm and happy inside.

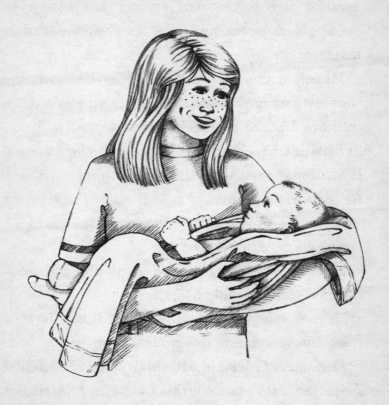

When Melanie's dad came home from work, her mother was waiting for him in the living room.

"George," she said. "I just can't handle this anymore."

Mr. Parker tossed his hat and briefcase on the

sofa. "What?" he quizzed.

"The housework and the baby—it's just too much for me."

Melanie's dad was puzzled. He shrugged his shoulders. "So what do you want to do about it?"

"I want to hire a babysitter."

"That's fine with me," George said, "as long as the sitter is good with children. I won't trust my son with just anyone."

"I have someone special in mind," said Mrs. Parker.

"Who?" asked her husband as he dropped into the easy chair. "Sandy Morgan?"

"Nope! George, meet our new babysitter." Mrs. Parker waved an arm toward the kitchen.

Out walked Melanie with Matthew in her arms. "Hi, Dad! Got your checkbook handy?" Melanie asked.

George Parker's eyes widened, and his mouth dropped open. The smile that flashed across his face equaled the ones he wore at the birth of his children—both of them.

Eleven

MELANIE'S tenth birthday celebration was the best party ever. The Parkers, George, Samantha, Melanie, and Matthew, were finally a family. Melanie felt so good, she even invited Tommy Watson to her party. And Tommy turned out to be only half a wimp. Melanie only had to slug him once when he said little Matthew needed more hair.

"I'm really happy," Melanie said after she blew out the candles on her birthday cake.

"What did you wish for?" Sandy Morgan asked.

"She's not supposed to tell," Tommy Watson answered, helping himself to a handful of candy.

"We'll have cake and ice cream after Melanie

opens her presents," Mrs. Parker announced.

The party guests all went into the living room where Melanie's presents were piled. Melanie sat on the carpet. She was glad she'd talked her mom out of making her wear a fancy dress. Her old jeans felt much more comfortable.

One by one Melanie unwrapped her gifts. Sandy gave her a T-shirt with a picture of Melanie's favorite rock group on it. Uncle Bill and Aunt Judy had sent their gift through the mail. It was a radio with headphones. Her parents gave her a neat new outfit. Even Tommy Watson gave her a nice present—a record album.

Soon all the presents had been opened. "There's still one present missing," Mr. Parker said to his daughter.

Melanie smiled but looked puzzled. "I have something from everybody. What's missing?"

"There's one more present. It's coming by special delivery," Mr. Parker told Melanie. He leaned close to his wife and whispered in her ear. "I just wish they'd hurry up and get here."

"Relax," Mrs. Parker whispered back as Matthew fidgeted in her arms. "I spoke to them on the phone yesterday. They'll be here."

Then as if right on cue, the doorball rang. Mr. Parker went to the window and looked out at the driveway. "It's them," he said. Turning to his daughter he added, "Answer the door, Melanie. It's the delivery man with your gift."

Melanie shrugged her shoulders and got up and walked to the door. What's the big mystery? she wondered as she opened the front door.

"Happy Birthday, freckle face!" It was Aunt Judy and Uncle Bill. "We have a special-delivery present for you!" they shouted before Melanie could utter a sound.

Aunt Judy held out her arms. In her hands was a fluffy white kitten.

Melanie's eyes widened in surprise. She was completely speechless. She turned to look at her parents.

"Well, take it," her father said. "The kitten is yours. It's one of Miss Kitty's babies."

"We cooked this up when learned Miss Kitty was going to have kittens," said Melanie's mom.

Melanie reached out and took the kitten from her aunt. The little kitten meowed. Tenderly, Melanie hugged the tiny fluff ball to her chest.

"But I thought I couldn't have a cat," Melanie said as she walked into the living room. "What about the nursery and the baby?"

"Oh, I think we can train a new kitten to stay out of the nursery," replied Mrs. Parker.

"If this kitten is half as smart as its mother, that will be easy," said Aunt Judy as she and Uncle Bill came in and sat down.

"Besides," added Mr. Parker as he winked at his daughter, "Matthew has a new babysitter to watch out for him now—and she's super!"

Melanie smiled proudly and stroked the kitten's soft fur. Holding the kitten gently, she walked over to her baby brother. She took his hand in hers and ran it down the kitten's back. "Matty," she said, "this kitten is my present, but it's our cat."

Everyone in the room applauded and began to sing another chorus of "Happy Birthday."

Melanie beamed and cuddled the kitten against her chest. "This was the best birthday ever," she said. Her baby brother squealed in delight as if to agree.

About the Author

MICHAEL PELLOWSKI was born January 24, 1949, in New Brunswick, New Jersey. He is a graduate of Rutgers, the State University of New Jersey, and has a degree in education. Before turning to writing he was a professional football player and then a high school teacher.

He is married to Judith Snyder Pellowski, his former high school sweetheart. They have three children, Morgan, Matthew, and Melanie, and two cats, Carrot and Spot.

Michael is the author of more than fifty books for children. He is also the host and producer of two local TV shows seen on cable TV in his home state. His show "Fun Stop," a children's comedy show, has been nominated as the best local cable TV children's show in America.